G. C. Smith

Pulling Back
The Covers

Cover Design: Brittany J. Jackson

Published by G Publishing, LLC

ISBN: 978-0-9834307-2-8

Library of Congress Control Number: 2011933264

Printed in the United States of America

Introduction

The workplace can be a strange and exciting place. We form friendships, develop relationships, and pretend to like those with whom we have nothing in common except maybe a paycheck. Although this is a work of fiction, each character in it should ring true to the reader: we have all worked with someone undeserving of a position, who is totally spastic, or who tries to overcompensate due to insecurities. We have also encountered others who exhibit more endearing traits.

These character sketches are meant to be glimpses only—snap-shots of people we might work with. We can never see the whole picture of those people; we often don't really know the person sitting next to us or the person who brings in the office treats. We *think* we know them, because we spend long hours in their company, share their tragedies and secrets, and offer them encouragement when they are having a bad day. Each person, whether a pain in the neck or a pleasure to be around, is remarkable as each provides insight and educates us in the importance of thinking for ourselves and realizing that life may not ever be fair and that sometimes we just have to walk away and start from scratch.

The events in this book dealing with my personal childhood experiences and my dance class are autobiographical. But everything else in the book is completely fictitious.

There is no education like the one you receive on the job. Despite their best efforts, no university or college can offer the hands-on experience one gets from a working beside a complete stranger. When you pull back the covers, you see glimpses of their true being and how they try to hide their true selves.

Chapter 1: Mama

I used to tell people I was born in Paris when, in all actuality; I lived on a street named Paris. I had a love-hate relationship with my house and at times was embarrassed by its appearance. It had no modern appliances and lacked rooms. You opened the front door and could immediately see the entire house from front to back. Once, I heard an old lady refer to it as a shotgun house. The living room was very small and consisted of a large sofa, small sofa, bar, and a heater that tried to keep us warm in the winter. We would often get dressed by the heater in the winter. Sometimes when it was very cold, my mother would turn on the stove and leave the oven door open to try to combat the drafts that blew through the house.

My mother had a knack for decorating and could make anything in that room appear large and in style. She kept plastic covers on the furniture as a means of protection. Later, I understood how important those pieces of plastic were. She used them to make things last longer. No matter how little she had, my mother did not believe in buying cheap, not when it came to anything you expected to use for a long time. Shoes, furniture, appliances were meant to last, and she stressed the importance of paying for what you get— that you got what you paid for.

The bedrooms were small and my sister's "room" consisted of a bed inside a room that could only hold a bed and should have been used as a closet. I always wondered why she did not suffer from claustrophobia. My room had a bed, window, and a large cabinet used to hold my clothes. I loved that room, and it was my hideaway and provided me with great joy at times. My mother's room was a wonder. She had vivid imagination and took pleasure in always changing her hair or her environment. Once, I came home from school to find her room painted black with black spots on the ceiling. It made the room feel large and cool at the same time.

The house did not have central heat or air, so it was very cold in the winter and really hot in the summer. Room air-conditioners and fans could not keep it cool, but somehow we survived. It was just the three of us. My mother, sister, and I lived in that house, and it was happy at times despite its appearances.

Education is learned, and the focus is life. I received my education off the back of my mother. She was gorgeous with a loud laugh and even louder voice. She was the one who taught me laughter, the art of cleanliness, and understanding. There is no better teacher than a great woman who understands and encourages you to be your best.

At an early age, I learned the importance of books and the power they held. As a young girl, I thought I was pretty hot stuff because I read books that had more than fifty pages. It happened because a neighbor the same age as I bragged how she read every day and challenged me to read more pages than she did. She was the catalyst who got me reading something every day. In high school, although I was not a great student (I was the one who kind of faded into the background), I carried on with my daily reading.

There was no sleeping in my mother's house if the kitchen was not clean. That meant no dishes in the sink, no trash on the floor, and no pots in the refrigerator. If you tried to sleep before these tasks were executed, you would awaken to the sound of "Get your ass up, and get that damn kitchen clean!" I often used to think that—as a sort-of second punishment—she purposely waited until you were in a deep sleep before she awakened you. Talk back, mumble, or attempt to roll your eyes, and you might have a split lip to go along with the ass whipping you were going to get. Ohh, the kitchen still got cleaned— with a hand to your lip, sleep deprivation, and fingers wrinkled from dish water.

This is how you cleaned the kitchen in my mama's home. A capful of bleach went into hot dish water so that the glasses or any other dishes were never greasy. The floors were always swept and mopped. We had no cabinets. Our one pantry consisted of a set of unenclosed wooden shelves about the size of a small dresser. The top shelf held flour, sugar, and other glass jars. The next shelf held an assortment of canned goods, and the last shelf was dedicated to holding pots and pans. This was how she made do with what she had. (I used to marvel at how people on television complained about no cabinet or shelf space. We absolutely did not have either one.)

You did not go to sleep if the rest of the house was not cleaned properly, either. Cleaning the bathroom meant scrubbing the toilet with bleach and an old rag. We had to make sure the screws around the toilet bowl were sparkling. Old toothbrushes, which we recycled as cleaning devises, were excellent for this task.

Next in importance after the cleanliness of the house was how you cooked and prepared foods. You never ever wanted to cook meat or vegetables unless you thoroughly washed it first. Cook some nasty-ass meat, and you were liable to get your ass chopped off much worse than what the cow had to endure to get your table. We always rinsed off the tops of canned goods before opening.

We never ever let clothes spill out of the hamper, and we always washed any new item of clothing before wearing it. She used to say, "We don't know who touched those damn clothes or what happened to them! Before you put them on your ass, you'll clean them!" She explained that clothes were handled by many people before they reached you and that the lady who tried on the pants or shirt before you might not have been too particular about deodorant or soap and water. Worse yet, she said, you wouldn't want to have boil your privates due to crabs—and I'm not talking about the kind that come out of the ocean.

Her wit and constant hammering of us about the importance of cleanliness prepared me for what I would have to endure and gave me the common sense I needed to work with those who are different. Many times, I miss that house!!!!

Chapter 2: School Years

We all have memories of our school years—grade school, middle school, high school, and beyond. Those of you who miss high school, pull out your yearbook and look at the pictures of yourself and those you called your friends. Ask yourself the following questions: Do you miss your body? How easy was your life during high school? Do you miss your friends? Do you miss the music and/or clothes? Lastly, would you go back to those days? If you answer yes to the last question, then you totally missed out on your education and the importance of learning to move on and progress in the world.

If you are like me, you remember bits and pieces of middle school and grade school but most of your memories are of high school. Ninth grade—you were so glad to be a part of the grown-up team, and everything was new and exciting. You began the high-school education process by wanting to be part of the club or the clique. That process also included wanting the latest fashions in jeans, shirts, and shoes. My family income was limited, which is a nice way of saying, we didn't have much of shit at times. But, when we did have money, my mother shared, and I learned the value of a dollar. If I could get 2 or 3 pairs of pants for $100.00, why spend it all on one. My friends came from two-parent middle-income homes and did not have to stretch money. They didn't always get what they wanted, but they did not understand the financial struggles of a single-parent family. To their credit, they never treated me differently or made me feel inferior. If one of us did not have money for something, then another would share, or we would change plans to do something less expensive. This is the kind of friendship one should have later in life— one in which money is not the most important thing.

The high-school years begin the transition into adulthood. And I learned many a lesson. Lesson number one: the importance of friendship and how being with the right person can open doors. I can remember the girl who was dumb as bricks, but, because her father knew a certain person, she passed, and graduated at the top of her class. She flunked out of her first year of college but went on to get a degree anyway (or so I heard).

Look at the person who routinely got into trouble but somehow manage to get into one of the best schools in the country. My favorite person was the one I labeled "the politician." This girl only spoke during election times. Believe it or not, she knew everyone by name. But, once she got into office, she forgot who elected her or the purpose of the election. If she went into politics, she could be president with her flair for uplifting, campaigning, and bull shitting.

Lesson number two: use what you got. Some people are natural beauties, both outwardly and inwardly. The rest of us make the most of what we have. We present a pretty package and perfect our techniques. We carefully plan our outfits, style our hair in various ways, apply make-up, and otherwise diminish our body flaws. Some people *added* to what they had. Those with small breasts stuffed their bras. (Now, plastic surgery has replaced stuffing—a damn shame for young girls.) You gotta do what you gotta do, especially if you're not naturally fit and trim. (I was not the girl who enjoyed playing sports. I don't mind exercising, when it is my choice, when I am not being graded or being chased by large animals.)

Lesson number three: be proud of yourself. I like how public schools have a blend of cultures, races, and socioeconomic backgrounds. This is real life—not the one you find in an exclusive private school where the only culture is green. Go to a public-school graduation, and then go to a private-school graduation. Pay attention to the mother who has tears running down her face or the father who is too choked up to speak. What obstacles did they have to overcome to make it? Look at the individual who has not one family member in the audience but manages to smile, take pictures, and bask in the glory of his accomplishments.

High school is also where I learned to curse and how to use words to my advantage. Thanks!!!

Chapter 3: College

Ahh, college! I went to college as what they called a nontraditional student, which is a nice way of saying "an old lady goes to school." But my college experience, aside from life's and my mother's education, was the best. That's where I learned education can be fun, especially if you have good professors.

One summer, I took a dance class. I needed an elective, and it was the only course I could take. As a nontraditional student, I had to embarrass myself in front of those who were younger and more dance savvy. The professor, whose name I cannot remember, was pleasant and understanding. After weeks of doing different moves, we took the final exam, which consisted of her calling out the learned moves. This was the scene. All the students were lined up outside the classroom, waiting to be called. You could not see in the room, nor could you hear. Once you completed your exam, you exited through the side door and could not reenter so as to give the waiting students a heads up. My heart was beating hard when she called out X (that's me). I opened the door.

"Are you ready?" she asked.

"Yes," I answered.

"I will call out the moves, and you will perform."

I was the first one she called. I performed with minimal embarrassment and thought this might not be so bad. Oh no, my next dance involved extending the arms and gracefully leaping across the room. What I performed looked liked a chicken skipping on ecstasy. Worse of all, I heard laughter and thought the other students were peeping at me. No, it was the professor. Not only was she laughing, she was trying very hard not to, which made it all the worse. This lady had tears running down her face. In between laughter, she kept apologizing and stated, "I am so sorry, but you are the first student, I ever laughed at, and please don't be offended." Was I offended? I am not sure, but I did get an A, which probably was based more on my determination than my artful dance moves. The teacher's reaction also reminded me that, yes, professors are human, and it is okay to laugh.

The professor who did not give a shit what you thought or felt was my favorite. She was not from the United States and made sure you knew it. She had a passion for her profession and a passion for children. If you earned her respect, you knew you were good. Piss her off, and look out. When I turned in my first paper to her, I was ballsy. I knew this was an A paper. *Ha!* She returned the paper with bold red lines across it and multiple notes in the margin. "Who asked your opinion?" she wrote on the side of one page. "How do you know? What is your supporting evidence? Are you sure?" Not only was I mad, but I thought she was a lunatic. I had the nerve to challenge her by stopping by her office (unannounced and not during scheduled student hours) to discuss my paper.

I greeted her. She did not respond. "What are these notations?" I inquired.

She took the paper from my hand and asked if I knew what college material looked like. Not only was I fuming but I ready to curse and trying hard not to. She began by shaking her head and then launched into a tirade. "Let me tell you something: no one cares about your opinion unless you have a position of power, money, and are an expert in the field or know what you are talking about. Since, you do not fall into any of those categories; write a paper which reflects facts that you can substantiate and don't mock me by writing the word 'I' repeatedly. You have one week to return your paper.

I returned it in less than a week, and she gave it right back, stating, "Use the whole time to perfect your paper, or you will fail my course."

I perfected the paper. She later told me she respected me for not giving up even though I did not earn an A from her nor would I receive one until I grasped the knowledge she presented and interpreted it accurately. She had to get the last word!

There was a professor who did not allow you to disrespect him or come to class late. I heard all sorts of stories about this man. The bottom line—he was about business. There was no escaping his class, as it was a requirement, and he was the only one who taught it. The first couple of classes went smoothly, but you knew someone had to try his hand. It started with the locked door. He did not like students walking in on the middle of his lecture, nor did he like for anyone to be late. He was twenty minutes into the lecture when the door opened. I sat up because I knew that this was going to be better than *Lifetime*.

Miss Jones walked in with pants that resemble pajamas, a tank top, and a scarf tied around her head. This was not her first time she had been late. He immediately stopped and inquired if she was on her way to a slumber party.

When she did not respond, he asked her if she knew what time the class began. Miss Jones responded with a "Yeah" and a neck roll.

"Class," he said in that eloquent voice of his, "Miss Jones has decided to join us from what appears to be a drunken slumber party. Now, you may thank her as we will have a pop quiz on what was presented in the first twenty minutes of class. Pull out a sheet of paper and answer these questions." After the quiz, he gave us a lecture on the importance of time and how your appearance rather intentionally or unintentionally defined who you are.

I was so green went I started college. The atmosphere was different; the professors a mixed bag of nuts, and the students were all over the place. Just like in high school, the same mix carried over into college. Except college brought out the true tramps. I had a summer course (something about summer courses makes me remember them more than winter courses) with two females who rarely came to class and hardly passed a test. One day, I asked if they had studied. (Yes, I was naïve.) They laughed in my face.

"Why the hell would I study when I have a vagina?"

"Excuse me?"

"Look," one told me, leaning into me with a top that had the seams holding hands to keep it together, "I never wear a top which fits, nor do I wear panties or pants on test day."

"Professors don't fall for that," I argued.

"Honey, a man is a man is a man." She passed with a higher grade than I.

The rest of my college years passed with a mixture of stress, excitement, and a feeling of ready-to-get-the-hell-on. During my last semester as a senior in the bachelor program, a kind and knowledgeable professor suggested that I apply for the master program, and he predicted I would go far. He saw my potential and encouraged it.

That program was hard, and the long non-paying internships did not make it any easier, but we prevailed. Those classes on ethics, social responsibility, politics, moral codes, and values often do not apply to many organizations that incorporate their own values and ideas regarding business and the delivery of services. Fortunately for many of us, the combination of upbringing and school prepares us for the education of surviving on the job with those who have no understanding of what is morally correct.

Chapter 4: Looking for a Job

If you are serious about looking for a job or even applying for one, never take a friend with you. On a summer day, a friend at the time asked me to take her to fill out an application at an organization she was dying to become a part of. I did not want to go, nor was I interested in applying, but she convinced me, and—surprise!—less than a month later, I was called in for an interview.

Was I happy? Hell, yes! I was 32 years old at the time, yet, with two degrees, my salary was $25,000.00 a year. Try telling a client who's making twice as much as you, yet working fewer hours, that it is better to go to school than stand on a street corner. After getting my stupid ass cursed out numerous times (client's exact words) and getting laughed at daily, I knew I needed to change venues.

The day I was called in for the interview, I was tired and cranky. I only had a few dollars, which I could use either for gas or lunch. I went for the gas and a cheap pack of thigh highs, which later on proved disastrous. I arrived early and met two very professional yet very different employees who, if I was hired, would become my co-workers. During the interview, I was asked a series of questions, and, I must admit, my answers were good. After this first interview, I went on to the next, and that is where the trouble began. During the second interview, I felt one of the thigh highs begin to lose its grip and proceed to slide down my leg. I knew, if I stood up, it would come down around my ankles, and I could not figure out a way to hold my leg, purse, and attaché case and shake hands at the same time. Luckily, the interviewer had to leave the office, and on the floor I spotted a rubber band which I eased up around my thigh. Thirty minutes later, my thigh began to look like a drum stick, and I was shaking with pain.

After the painful interview, I was told to report to Human Resources. In pain and limping, I went to my parked car and slid the grippers off both legs. At that point, I was offered the job and a salary increase of $10,000.00 more than what I was making in my present position. I was so happy; I was walking on air and making plans about how to utilize my increase in status. Oh, one important factor I forgot to mention—the job involved working with the mentally ill and the chronic substance abuser. Having worked with both populations during my internship and college years, I theorized that this would be a breeze. However, I was very naive; I was sure that the people I would come in contact with would be nothing like those I saw on TV. Wrong!! TV could never prepare you for real life, real attitudes and real personalities.

After orientation (which I won't bore you with the details of), I began my first official day on the job and met with several surprises. The first involved keys. Every door on the unit was locked. That included bathrooms, which you could only enter via a key. *What in the hell have I gotten myself into?* I wondered. My next surprise came when I met my immediate supervisor, who had been out when I was hired. Whatever picture you have in mind of a supervisor, immediately erase it and replace it with this image: Alex was big and flamboyant. He wore muscle shirts no one his size should ever wear. (What not to wear was not a part of his vocabulary.) He also had the bad habit of using words which irritated the hell out me.

Our initial meeting took place while he was eating lunch, and his main focus involved his hot wings and fries.

"Come in! Come in!" he gestured. "It is nice to meet you; have a seat and tell me a little about yourself."

"I have a bachelor's degree in Social Work and a Master's in Social Work Administration."

"Did you like your previous job?" asked Alex.

At first, I couldn't answer because he had distracted me by inserting a whole wing into his mouth and removing only the bone. *Damn!* "Y-yes," I stammered.

"Do you know what population you will be serving here?" "I was told I would be working with the mentally ill and those addicted to alcohol and drugs."

"Mm," he grunted and replied, "I don't believe in micro-managing, yet I know everything that goes in the building, because those around me will keep me informed." I simply nodded. "You certainly have the educational expertise, but it's the ground work which either kills you or makes you a really good counselor."

"But I'm not a counselor."

He inserted another chicken wing and shrugged, "Who cares?"

Talking around a mouthful of food, he sent me home.

I needed to rest to prepare myself mentally for the upcoming challenges I had to face. To say my encounter with Alex was the strangest meeting would be a lie because I had many more to come.

Chapter 5: My First Professional Job—and Liz

This was the beginning of my true education, of understanding that you see above the covers is not necessarily what is under the covers.

Liz was mellow, calm, and even tempered—but, piss her off, and that was it. She could deliver stingers that would bring tears to your eyes and make you wish you had never opened your mouth. Each shift had a nurse, who, due to education, experience, and management skills, was labeled charge nurse. I was told that, at one time, charge nurses got extra pay, but now it was just a title. Someone forgot to tell Liz. When I was brought onto the unit, she walked over gave me a hug and said, "I'm glad they finally hired someone young and educated." I laughed, and she took my arm and barked over her shoulder, "I'm showing her the ropes."

She took me to the exam room, locked the door, and lit a cigarette. I looked around nervously and she laughed in that deep voice of hers and told me, "Don't worry; I turned on the fan. Plus, you can't smell the smoke in the hallway. Now," she said in between smokes, "let me give you a lesson on how things work around here. Alex is just the figurehead. He is hardly here, but he has spies everywhere, and he has the gift of gab. His nickname is snap dragon." She must have read the confusion on my face because she waved her hand in answer and continued. "His spies are the people he promoted and gave phony raises to. You have two choices, my dear. Suck up and try to get in good with him and his crowd or do what you are paid to do, stay the course, and forget about trying to make friends. I've been here for twenty years and know too many secrets for the bastards to try and get rid of me. I know who's sleeping with whom, who's addicted, who's in debt, and why they can't afford to leave their job."

"Why are you telling me this? I asked.

"I told you. I like you, and you seem smart." She put the cigarette out on the heel of her shoe and bent to wipe up the ashes she had let fall to the floor. Making sure the cigarette was out; she placed the wadded mess in her lab coat pocket. "Now, listen," she said pointing her finger in my face." "Those two you'll be working with don't know jack. Both were hired based on family relations, if you know what I mean. Every day we have what is called a treatment team meeting. It's comprised of the doctor, the therapists, discharge planners, the nurse, and the patient. The purpose is to set goals and methods of treatment for patients, but often it turns into a bitch session. You are the facilitator."

"Excuse me?" I said. "That's your job—to make

sure the patient has everything they need to be discharge from the hospital."

"How is that my job?"

"Don't be dumb," she said." Opening the door, she beckoned me with her finger, and, locking the door, she gave me a wink.

"Are you ever afraid of the patients?" I asked.

"Honey, she said with a smile, "it ain't the patients you have to worry about."

I walked back onto the unit, thinking about our intense conversation. I sat down to read patients' charts to get a better understanding of what I was to encounter and to give myself their history to better understand what brought them into the hospital. Meanwhile, Liz had snuck out to her car to smoke in peace. As a nurse, she knew her addiction was bad, but she couldn't stop herself, even though her mother had died of cancer and her sister had survived breast cancer. She thought of these things even as she lit her next cigarette.

While Liz portrayed herself as strong and wise, she had areas in her life which were weak, weak, weak. Liz had several secrets of her own, which were dreadful and nasty. Liz never told her husband the big secret she had held within for years and years, nor did she tell her husband she knew of the affair he'd been having for the past ten years with a woman ten years younger than Liz. She kept quite because she liked the home life and the idea of not having to work too hard and not having to worry who was going to pay the mortgage or if it could be paid. Liz prided herself on telling others, "What is done in the dark will see the light," but that was the very advice that she doled out to others that she missed for herself. She kept on smoking through two cigarettes, and then she sprayed herself and returned to the unit

By the time my first day ended. I was very tired and stressed. I came home, stripped, took a hot bath, and fell asleep before 8:00 p.m.

The second day on the job, I was presented to my officemates. There was a total of four of us in one office, and one person was a loudmouth who went on and on until I just wanted to scream, "Shut the fuck up!" I went from making a little bit of money with my own private office and bathroom to making more money with a shared office and bathroom. Damn!

That morning, I attended my first staff meeting, and it was a crazy. Nothing was prepared, half the staff was late, and they seemed to lack a leader. Who the hell wanted to spend an hour trapped in a mess like this? I looked around the room at the mixed and unhappy expressions. Some seemed to have a couldn't-care-less look on their faces like "Whatever," and others appeared to be thinking about what was for lunch. I was somewhere in between. Finally, after fifteen minutes, Alex walked in, and immediately some of the posture in the room changed.

"We have a new face" said, Alex and asked everyone to introduce themselves to me. The lady sitting closest to her gave her name as Hilary, and her title was therapist. The next person was Charles, who was a counselor. Megan was a discharge planner (someone who made sure patients had housing, support systems, and resources for medications). Rounding out the room was Liz. After the introductions, Alex slid a giant box of doughnuts, which he had carried in, to the middle of the table.

After the meeting, Liz grabbed my arm and pulled me aside. "Well," she said, "How did you like it?"

"Well," I said, imitating her lead, "I can't form an opinion based on one meeting!" This was not entirely untrue, but, having just met her, I was not comfortable divulging things to her. Especially since I was new and she came off as being bossy— something that grated on my nerves since I hated to be bossed around. Liz laughed and told me she'd be back.

Liz exited the building, stood next to the trash bin, and lit her extension to her arm. Smoking calmly, she noticed security approaching and greeted the guard by name. "Hi, Bert," she said.

"Liz," he replied in a greeting, stretching out the syllable of her name. "Now, you know that ya shouldn't be smokin'."

Liz smiled and kept smoking. He shook his head and entered the building. Liz continued to smoke and thought to herself what he should do with his ideas about her smoking. Never mind the fact that she knew without a doubt she was breaking the rules and policies.

She finished her cigarette and turned to go to into the building when she noticed someone coming across the parking lot. It was Charles, the counselor. She waited for him to cross the street and noticed that, when he spotted her, he slowed his walk. When he finally reached her, she asked where he'd disappeared to so fast.

"Nowhere," he replied, trying to get around her.

"Then, if it's nowhere, you should have been in the building."

"Is there some work I'm missing?"

"Yes, there's some work you're missing," she replied in a sly manner. He slinked passed her, and she proceeded to follow him until she was interrupted by the vibration of her cell phone. Looking at the Caller ID, she sighed heavily and flipped open the phone. "Yes?" she said, instead of "Hello."

"I have to work late tonight," said the voice which belonged to her husband.

"How late?"

"Late" was the reply before he hung the phone. Liz slammed the phone shut and told herself not to dwell on what he would be doing and with whom. He always called her even if the excuse was lame. She had to give him credit for one thing: He never had a baby with the witch!

Her phone vibrated again, and, this time, she did not look at the caller I.D. before she answered it. "Yes?"

"Is this is Elizabeth?" asked the caller

"Who's calling?"

"This is Ann, your husband's girlfriend, and we

need to talk."

"*Talk?*"

"I don't want to do this over the phone, and I don't want this to turn into a cat fight over a man who, I feel, has made his choice."

"Are you out of your fuck-ass mind?" asked Liz "You have the nerve to call me and make demands on my life."

"Look." said the caller, stressing the syllables in *look*, "I want to do this in a civilized manner, and I think the best thing is for one of us to pursue her life of happiness while the other exits gracefully. I think that should be you."

"And I think you should kiss the four corners of my ass and wish me a happy birthday!" With that, Liz slapped her phone shut and marched into the building—and this time she made it into the unit uninterrupted. *The nerve of that skitch!* Liz, loved calling women whom she did not like *skitches*. It was a name she made up. It meant a bitch with an itch, and she could not think of anything nastier.

Liz did that all her life—made up stories and names for people. Her formative years were happy for her but must have looked dysfunctional to anyone watching from the outside. Liz was the product of a rape by an uncle, whom she saw once at a family gathering when he introduced himself as her father and uncle. He was drunk at the time and thought it was funny until an aunt overheard the conversation and enlisted her brothers to beat his ass to a pulp and put what was left of it on a bus to parts unknown. Liz never saw him again. Her mother—who at the time Liz was born was only 15—was unable to care for her so, an older cousin raised Liz. Maybe, because she felt sorry for Liz, knowing the child's unfortunate background, or maybe because she truly loved the little girl, she spoiled Liz and made sure Liz was told on a daily basis how much she was loved and how much she belonged in this world. Liz's birth mother developed more of a sisterly relationship with Liz rather than a mother-daughter bond. She was very festive and pretty and had a knack for catching the eyes of men. She never worked a day in her life and spent money like water on lavish clothes, perfume, purses, and accessories. Liz feared she would end up having to take care of her in her old age

When Liz's mother came to town, she and Liz would sit up late drinking and talking about men. It was something that Liz's husband did not approve of, nor did he understand. He thought there should be strict divisons between what children and their parents did together. He thought there should be strict divisions for everything but Liz liked to experiment, and she had no fear of the rules.

Chapter 6: Jimmy, the Call-in Man

Jimmy was a hard worker—when he appeared for work. He was funny and energetic, and his co-workers loved working with him because he made the shift go by faster. He was the only male nurse, and the female nurses appreciated him, for he could usually calm a psychotic patient with a look or calm manner. When calmness did not work, it helped that Jimmy was over 6'2" and solidly built. Jimmy should have been in sales, as he could sell you anything; you would walk away smiling, glad you had the chance to interact with him. This was fine most days, but the times Jimmy called in drove the administrator crazy because she had to call people at home and beg them to come in to cover. If someone had already worked a shift, this meant overtime—something that was frowned upon.

Jimmy always had excuses for his absences: they ranged from the deaths of pets or friends to car trouble, burglary, capsized boat (no one questioned how he had managed to call from the water, if his boat was capsized), stomach ailments, the need to renew his license, and the break-up of relationships.

Jimmy could get girls, but he apparently could not manage to keep them; judging by his many absences, something always went wrong. People wondered where he went and why he called in, but they would dismiss it as Jimmy just being Jimmy.

The times I met with Jimmy, something always appeared to be off with him—as if he could not calm down or look me straight in the eye. He would tell outlandish stories, but he would not laugh. If he did, his laughter seemed false, forced. I worried about him and voiced my concerns to Alex, who told me I had no reason to be concerned. Okay, then. I wouldn't be concerned. I suspected what Jimmy's problem was, but I did not want to state it aloud or cast suspicion where none was due. Of course this did not make me feel better nor did it make the situation better. Jimmy continued to call in until one day he was caught in the parking lot.

Jimmy, like others who smoked, would sneak outside to his car or off campus to smoke. Jimmy was supposed to return to the building after his break but he didn't. The nurses became concerned when he was gone for over an hour. They did not want to report him because they knew he would receive a reprimand for abandoning his station, but, being shorthanded, they fell behind in distributing patients' medications and getting them settled for the evening meal. Finally when it was going into the second hour and they were stretched thin, he appeared with flowers and an apology. He had been so tired, he said, that he fell asleep in his car. No one in management or any other staff members knew of the incident, and I did not find out until much later.

Jimmy was faking happiness—something that was spelled out when a very psychotic patient pointed to him and stated in moment of clarity, "You need to be with me taking meds." I remember being told that, no matter how psychotic or delusional a person may be, there are always those moments when they speak the truth. Jimmy was fooling his colleagues, but he was not fooling the patients. Another incident occurred: Jimmy was found asleep in a patient's bed next to the patient! But the staff member who found him accepted his excuse that he had been tired and was starting new medication which disoriented him. The staff member should have written him up but did not, and the patient was too psychotic to understand what had happened.

Loneliness was a part of Jimmy's life. He could not keep a relationship, and he had little contact with family or friends. He neglected his job to go take care of his selfish needs. Jimmy was a chronic and severe alcoholic. That is why is he called in so frequently and left his post several times. He could not control himself, and lately it was becoming more and more obvious.

One Thursday, when he did manage to drag himself into work, he reeked of straight liquor. Liz noticed it and dragged him into a closed office. She asked him if he had been drinking. He denied it—in words so slurred that they confirmed it.

"I'm not going to ask you again," said Liz."

"No, no, no," said Jimmy. Then he burst out laughing and started to tell a joke.

"I am not going to let you back out onto the floor. It's not safe for you or the patients. Do you understand what I am saying, Jimmy?"

He began to cry, and Liz, feeling bad for him and his situation, patted his back and tried to reassure him.

After a few minutes, he was able to pull himself together and asked what would happen next. Liz, being honest, replied that she was going to report this incident and suggested that it would be best if he asked for help instead of having it forced upon him. She also told him that she would not let him drive home.

Jimmy sat in silence as Liz made the necessary phone calls and at the last moment stated he was going home. Liz told him he was not driving and asked for his keys. He refused. Liz became scared that the argument might get physical because Jimmy was starting to get fidgety and nervous. Looking at her, he said, "I won't hurt you, but I am going home."

"Let me drive you. Please."

Jimmy gave her his car keys, and Liz went into the nurses' station to inquire if the Jimmy's replacement had made it in. Seeing his replacement was already there, Liz informed her that Jimmy was not feeling good and she was going to drive him home. She told her that she had her cell phone with her and could be reached if anyone had any questions. As soon as she took Jimmy home, Liz promised to return and help out. Officially, her shift had ended, but she had to file her report, and she did not want to leave things unattended. Liz had tried to reach Alex several times but was unable to, even though he was on call. She left a message requesting a return call as soon as possible but did not go into details.

Liz and Jimmy rode in silence after he gave directions on how to reach his home. Upon reaching his complex, he got out without a word to Liz. She noticed how haggard he looked and how his gait was unsteady and berated herself for not seeing before what she now saw. Following him into the apartment, Liz looked around in shock. Clothes were on the floor; empty bottles were on the floor; the place had an odor; and the TV was on. Liz went to turn off TV, but he stopped her. "I can't stand silence."

The place had an open view and, from the living room, Liz could see the entire layout, which consisted of a living room, kitchen, bedroom, and bath. "Go take a shower." Jimmy moved towards the bath, and Liz went into the kitchen to make coffee, but she did not believe in cooking in filth, so first she began to pick up the trash and his clothes. She opened several cabinet doors before she found his limited cleaning supplies. After she picked up the trash, she sprayed down everything with Lysol, include the TV remote and the doorknobs. Liz found the coffee in the refrigerator, but she did not find any other sources of food. No butter, no frozen dinners—not even ice. If he had any other sources for booze, they were well hidden. Either that, or he had drunk them all up.

After a long time, during which Liz began to worry about him, Jimmy finally came out of the bathroom. "Who does take out?" she asked him. He pointed to some menus near the TV and Liz chose Chinese food. He silently handed her the phone, and she placed the order. Jimmy sat down, and Liz gave him a cup of coffee. With shaking hands, he told her, "Thank you."

Liz used the phone again to call for a taxi. The food arrived five minutes before her taxi. She paid for the food and encouraged Jimmy to eat. He claimed he wasn't hungry, so she placed the bags on top of his stove.

They sat in silence until the taxi blew its horn. Jimmy tried to make a joke but then stopped and vowed that he would do what was needed and seek help.

Liz never saw Jimmy again. That was his last night working at the hospital. He continued to drink and lost his nursing license. He kept on this path for the next year until he got arrested for driving while intoxicated. Jimmy was forced into treatment, stayed sober for 41 days, and then returned to drinking. He continued to drink, even when he found himself sitting on a dirty mattress in a pay-by-the-day motel with no memories of the previous day or night and a swollen lip. Jimmy started crying while watching TV and looked for a bottle that was not there.

Jimmy attempted multiple times to achieve sobriety, including joining A.A. and undergoing court-ordered treatment, but the loss of his job and license was the last straw, and he seemed to lose all hope. He left the city and traveled as a beggar, sometimes a thief, but always an alcoholic.

Liz, never breathed a word to the other staff members who wondered and gossiped about what might have happened. She completed her paperwork, followed protocol, and kept her mouth shut.

Chapter 7: Charles, the Family Man

Charles, or Chuck as he was known, was nicknamed the family man. All he did all day long was brag about his family. It was either how smart they were or how beautiful his girls were. Charles met the girl of his dreams when he was a quarterback for his college football team. He spotted his future wife, Georgette, when she passed by him in a crowded bookstore. After he asked her out on a first date and they had a second and a third, she admitted she had orchestrated the bookstore encounter.

To the outside world, his family was his life, and they were perfect. Charles' boy was nicknamed "Smarts" by his co-workers because Charles always started each sentence with, "That boy is so smart." His daughter was the talented one. Everyone within the organization knew that she was excellent at tap dancing, and singing in the school's choir. Charles was proud, proud, proud of his family. His bragging made others around him want to choke him, and many times they avoided him to keep from hearing stories about his home life. But, when he had a captive audience—usually during a meeting, where there was no escape—he went on and on and on.

Charles was slick. He had a secret which he went to grave lengths to keep from his co-workers, friends, and family. You see, that beauty of a wife of his was no beauty—never had been and never would be. Her mood and attitude were nasty and got nastier every year when the New Year rolled around and she did not get what she wanted. He argued with her daily over why she didn't join Jenny Craig and why she just let herself go. To piss him off, she would deliberately smack her lips while eating and make moaning noises. She could not stand to look at Charles and resented the life he had force her to live. Her older sister married Mr. Corporate, and now they lived in a five-bedroom home with no children. She and Chuck and their kids lived in a three-bedroom home which was always messy. Clothes remained in the basket until it was time to iron. This meant, usually, the ironing was done at 6:00 in the morning before school and work. Mail was stacked on the dining room table along with magazines, books, knitting material, ribbons, and their oldest baseball glove. The only thing she kept clean were the dishes; she always made sure they were washed because she had a deep fear of roaches.

Charles was stuck with her because he could not afford to leave her due to the alimony and child support he would have to pay. He was miserable, and he did not want to think about his non-existent sex life with his spouse. He remembered when he was young and sexy with a head full of hair and had a different girl every week. His first year of marriage was great, but then the change happened, and he had to beg like a dog for sex. After a while, it got to a point where he didn't want the damn sex. Especially when she got undressed and her ass sagged and rippled like the waves in the ocean. And he couldn't stand those kids of his. The daughter stared at herself in the mirror all day and talked on the phone constantly to her friends. He felt sorry for her; she had her mother's genes and no hopes of ever getting an educational scholarship. His son, on the other hand, was bright but thought he knew everything. Whenever Charles approached him, he would snapp out answers or look at him as if Charles embarrassed him. Charles remembered his son's last ball game, when he asked his mother to wait in the van and told his father not to show up. If Charles did show, his son promised he would lose on purpose. Yeah, Charles had the perfect life of hell.

That was why Charles did what he did to relieve himself, and he had a plan to get out of his hell real soon. After years of daydreaming and months of planning, he could finally see a little tiny piece of the island over the ripples in the ocean.

Each day, Charles would sneak away and meet with clients. He got the idea to do so one day when a patient asked him why he wasn't in private practice. Charles realized how much more money he could make, and his wife would be none the wiser because the checks would all be made out to him. It took him three months of not eating lunch to be able to afford a two-room office and a bathroom he shared with other occupants of the building, but he was happy. To make sure he was not doing anything unethical, he would not accept anyone who was a patient at the hospital, but Charles' ethics did not cause him to believe that stealing time was unethical. On average, he would see at least four clients daily, whom he billed for seventy five dollars an hour. He took two-hour lunches and at various times of the day would disappear. When people inquired after his whereabouts, he always had a quick reply, whether it was a lie or the truth.

His business was good, and he knew he had to make his getaway soon, since word-of-mouth was beginning to spread and he did not want Georgette to know how much money he was making. To keep it all hidden, he kept his money in a safe he hid in the attic. Georgette would never take her ass into the attic, and the kids were scared of spiders and dark places. Every time, he thought about his deeds he laughed. Before long, he would be able to afford a real beauty queen, and he would bring her to parties and out to dinner in the middle of the city where everyone would wonder what Charles' profession was and how he was able keep a woman like that happy.

He was jolted out of his dreams by the ringing of his cell phone. He had programmed it to ring to the tune of *Law & Order* when his spouse called because, secretly, he had her pegged as the bad girl the D.A. was going to nail.

"Hello," he said, in that tired, slow voice of his.

"Is this how you answer the phone when your wife calls?"

"What do you want?"

"I need for you to stop by the grocery store on the way home because we are out of snacks—and did you pay the cable bill?"

"I haven't had time, and we don't need any snacks for the house." Getting bolder, Charles continued, "From now on, we are going to eat healthier, and that includes fresh fruit and vegetables."

His wife burst out laughing. "Fine! I'll wait until you get home, and then I'll go to the store. I don't feel like dragging the kids with me. What time will you leave?"

"I'll pay the cable bill over the phone, and I'll get home around six or six thirty, he said."

"Make it six," and she hung up."

Charles looks at the phone, and then he pulled his pants away from his stomach to peak inside his boxers. Yep, he still had 'em. Two, if anybody's counting. He wished he could leave her today. From his pocket, he extracted a scratch sheet of paper and began to write. After completing his thought, he pulled out his cell phone and pressed a number. When the voice answered, he stated, "We need to meet," and, without waiting for a response, he disconnected.

Chapter 7: Alex, the Ass

Alex loved to eat; there was no doubt about it. But, besides food, his greatest addiction was his husband, Donald. Donald married him because of the money he had inherited. He pursued Alex and convinced him that he was handsome and smart. He knew how Alex looked without any clothes on and that, no matter how much he paid for an outfit, it was ill fitting on him. What Alex lacked in looks he made up for it in other areas. No, he was not smart, but he had common sense and enough sense to put people in positions to make him look good at all costs.

Donald was no good and proved it over and over. He pawned the title to Alex's vehicle on more than one occasion, took out credit cards in his name, and then maxed out the limit. Yet, for some reason, Alex continued to forgive him and continued to stay in a marriage which he knew was loveless and even filled with contempt. Donald was gorgeous. He had a winning smile and a gorgeous, smooth completion. Those who met Donald could not understand the attraction between him and Alex. No matter how you felt about gay marriage in general, you would have to conclude that theirs in particular simply could not work.

Alex sat in his office wearing a pair of black pants so tight that you could see the imprint of his ass crack. He had on a tight blue shirt with little sharks on it and sported blue shoes. He thought the shoes brought out the color in his shirt. His thoughts were drifting to Donald. He had a mountain of paper work to do, but he did not know how to do it. nor did he feel like making an attempt to fake it. Looking at his watch, he noticed it was 11:00 a.m. *Close enough*, he thought. Alex buzzed his secretary and asked her if she wanted anything to eat. She said no. Alex told her he would be back in 30 minutes and to take down any phone messages.

On the way to his car, he saw Donald, waving at him to get his attention. For once, Alex wanted to pretend he did not see Donald. "What do you want, Donald, and how much is it going to cost me?"

"Why the attitude, Al?" Alex hated to be called Al, and Donald knew it. "Look," he said, "I need to get about twenty dollars from you."

Gazing at Donald with contempt, Alex struggled to get a bill out of his pocket and pulled out a twenty. He silently handed it to Donald. "Thanks, hon,: Donald said, giving him a peck on the cheek.

Bastard, Alex thought and, without giving Donald another thought, went in pursuit of his food.

He loved the restaurant that served the pasta. Today he wanted the shrimp and sausage with a slice of lemon cake. He was not one of those who minded eating alone. In fact, he relished and even enjoyed it. It gave him time to observe others and to think. Especially about his employees who all thought they were fooling him. He knew about Charles and his trifling ways and Liz's weakness. He also knew that his employees despised him. But he did not mind, nor did he care. It was all about the business and appearances. As long as the powers that be thought he was doing a good job, then the hell with what everybody else thought.

Alex's best asset was Liz because he could get Liz to do whatever he wanted when he wanted, and all he had to do was twirl her finger. He did not need to say which finger.

Reversing his thoughts as was his habit, he thought back to Donald and decided to put him on a budget. Donald had one month to obtain employment. If Donald would not agree and stop with the nasty comments, then he was revamping his life without Donald!

Alex's daydream was interrupted by his husband who slid into the booth next to him. "Hi, Al."

"Why did I marry you?" Alex asked.

"Because," Donald countered, I'm the only one who would look at you more than once."

"That used to bother me," Alex said, "but now I have just become immune to your nasty little slams at me—against my weight, looks, body, or money."

"But," said Donald, "you know you need me."

"And what about you, Donald? You need me. If

you left, you would have to get a job—or do you think that you are so attractive men will line up to support you and your nasty habits? Let's end this," said Alex.

Donald laughed out loud, and others turned to look at him, including a few women, who smiled. "No," said Donald "you don't want to end this, and neither do I. I can't live without you, and you cannot live without me. We are a perfect match made in hell!" With that, he got up and left, but not before whispering in the waitress's ear and enclosing twenty dollars in her hand. That was another problem with Donald—he attracted men and women.

Unfortunately, Alex's grandmother had stipulated in the trust that Alex had to be married by a certain age. She did not specify to whom, and it would never have dawned on her that it would have been a same-sex marriage. Alex's family was dismayed by his marriage, but they came to accept Donald.

Interrupting his thoughts, the waitress walked over to Alex's table and, smiling, said, "The nice man ordered a dessert for you and told you to enjoy your snack." Without missing a beat, Alex stated, "Bring me a slice of lemon cake."

Chapter 8: Hilary, the Crier

Hilary was the first therapist I met who needed a therapist herself. She spent many days leaving work and heading to her therapist office. She vented and voiced resentment against her colleagues and family.

Hilary had the nickname of crybaby. Her family used the name to teach her and to get her do to do their bidding. Hilary was born the last of six children, and her family was an odd mix of loudness and quietness. Her mother was shy and very dependent on her father. Hilary's mother did not voice an independent thought, not ever. Her father was loud and often rude. Women were made to feel less than a man, and he treated them as so. Hilary had two brothers and three sisters. All were married except for her and one brother who was going through a nasty divorce and residing in the basement of her sister Joyce's home. Hilary did not harbor any desire to get married and or have children but she did have a deep fear of being poor and under the control of others.

Truth be told, Hilary could not have any children due to the many abortions she had. She was not vocal or independent enough to insist on birth control from her partners, and she always forgot to take the pill or get the shot or something.

She was pleasant but afraid to voice her opinions, which when she was prompted to give them, proved to be valid and on point. In private Hillary could be found talking to herself, and, yes, she did answer. Her co-workers took advantage of her by asking her to work late, giving her the most difficult clients, and never including her in the fun activities unless, they wanted her to work or take the brunt of criticism from management, but she was beginning to get tired, and, when a mouse gets tired, it can turn into a rat.

Hilary came into her office, and in her mind she slammed the door, but in reality she did not. She was tired, and she wanted out of her job, but she could not afford to leave because she owed a brickload of student loans, and the possibility of not having a roof over her head scared her shitless.

The knock on her door made her jump.

She opened the door and was surprised to see the person standing on the other side.

"Are you busy?"

"No," said Hillary, opening the door wider to let the person in.

"I need a favor"

"I'm all out of favors," replied Hilary in her usual timid voice. Then, feeling stronger, she stated, "No, I can't do any favors."

"Even if it involves more money and a chance for you to leave?"

"How do you know I want to leave?"

"Because I want the same thing," said Charles, closing the door.

I'm going to let you in on a big secret, and I want you to promise that you will not tell a soul. I've been seeing patients every day for months, and I need a partner."

"Getting a divorce?" asked Hillary, not knowing how close she came to the truth.

"I am not getting divorced," Charles claimed. Hillary just gave him a look, and he smiled. "You know, I always thought you were a lot smarter than what you gave yourself credit for."

Hilary turned her back and began a silent conversation with herself. *You can do this*, said the voice, *and no one will find out. Plus, the extra money will carry you out of this atmosphere of people you dislike.*

"Hey, Hilary," said Charles, snapping his fingers in her face.

Sitting down in shock, Hilary asked, "How much are you charging by the hour?"

"Seventy five dollars."

"You need to increase the price to one hundred per hour and make sure you are seeing more than one person in the hour."

"What?"

"You know," Hilary explained in her small voice, "you can bill for an hour but only meet with a person for forty five minutes."

"Great!" said Charles, getting excited, "Can I trust you?"

"Can I trust *you*?"

At the same time, they both replied, "Yes."

Closing the door after Charles left, Hilary began to smile. She was the best counselor they ever had. She would always advocate for the client, no matter how timid or shy she was regarding her own feelings or thoughts. She was also no fool. Charles picked her after watching to make sure she did not talk too much, disclose secrets, or have any friends. Hilary was adept at watching people, and she watched her co-workers. Some she envied and some she hated.

She had also watched Charles when no one was looking, and she knew he crept away to see clients. He was not a good counselor, but he had the gift of gab, and he played up his assets to the hilt. She also knew Charles did not have any compunction about using her to suit his purposes. She had to keep talking to herself to remind herself not to get close to him and not to let him notice how attracted she was to him. Her emotions were in turmoil. Whenever she was advising clients, she would steer them *away* from a turmoil relationship. But, Hilary needed a man, and she needed one bad. The last time she was in a relationship, she pursued and harassed the man so much that he left the state and told her she need psychiatric help. Not a good thing for a counselor.

She did not like or trust Charles, but he was able to give her what she required in her time of need. On the other hand, she was still afraid of losing her job. *What to do?* she pondered.

Chapter 9: Charles's Divorce

Several days after meeting with Hilary, Charles found an attorney and proceeded with his plan to divorce Georgette. So as not to lose any business, he did at a time when he did not have clients booked, and he blew off a family meeting at work by telling the nurse the family did not want to meet when in all actuality it was he who did not want to meet with them. His lawyer was good, and he was also someone who had gone through a divorce a couple years ago. Charles had the knack for picking out people who had character flaws that he could exploit. He was just that type of snake. He requested the lawyer serve the papers immediately.

After taking almost all of the day, Charles met with Hilary to finalize his plans, then he got some boxes out of the hallway and loaded them up on his truck. He went back into his office and typed out his resignation. That is why he needed Hilary. He wanted her to be the fall-back person in case people asked about his new employment. He was opening his practice, but he did not want to have a paper trail. Hilary would cover for him. He also knew Georgette would be too lazy and too stupid to look for any hidden agendas, but, just in case, he wanted to cover his bases.

Outside in the sun, Charles looked at the sky and began to dance. He had no movement or rhythm, but he felt as if his toes were light as air. He hadn't been this happy since he was a child. All he had worked for was finally happening. "I'm free!" he shouted in the parking lot and jumped in the air. This was it!

Chapter 10: Dr. Riley

Dr. Riley was the best. He knew medicine, and he knew what was best for the patient whether they liked it or not or whether they wanted it or not. He knew how to cajole and get the truth out of those who would not take medicines and could always determine who was faking to avoid imprisonment or other legalities. He was arrogant, opinionated, and hot tempered. He didn't give a damn. He brought the hospital thousands and thousands of dollars in revenue, and his patients not only sought treatment from him but, because of him, sought treatment from his colleagues. The nurses hated and feared Dr. Riley. If necessary, to prove a point, he would berate them in front of other staff members and patients . Those who questioned him found themselves on the other side of the unemployment aisle.

Although he was brusque, he never stopped trying to help his patients, and, many times, he would call an insurance company himself to get the medications people needed. With a patient, he appeared uncaring, but he would take the time to explain the importance of diet and medication compliance. He also would call family and support systems to offer advice about how to care for a loved one with a mental illness. Nobody but those he treated ever saw this side of his personality, and they had an unwavering attachment to him because he helped them get better.

Alex was afraid of him and gave him anything he wanted but mostly he stayed out of his way. Dr. Riley had an aversion to men like Alex (lazy), and he did not try to hide it. He recently went to the president of the board and demanded Alex be let go before the end of the year. He had no doubt that his request would be acceded to and that he would have a choice in selecting Alex's successor.

For those looking in, no would have guess that Dr. Riley was not a privileged member of society or that he hadn't been wealthy all of his life. In fact, he had obtained his money and position by working hard and investing wisely. He married his first wife for her name and status. Her wealth did not hurt, but, when he found out that she could not have children, he divorced her after three years of marriage and walked away with half-a-million dollars since they did not have a prenuptial agreement. When he married again, Dr. Riley did not make the mistake his first wife had. His second wife had to sign a prenup stating that, if they divorced, she would get only what she brought into the marriage.

His current wife was considerably younger than he and did not have the status of his first wife, but he was able to mold her, and she did as she was told without question since he gave her mother several hundred dollars a month to supplement her income. He did not do it as a good deed but rather so he could brag about it and look good in the eyes of their friends who thought he was wonderful to ensure his mother in law lived comfortably. Dr. Riley did not give a damn about her comforts. A secret he tried to guard was that he was one cheap son of a bitch. His wife, Gloria, was given a monthly budget, and she had to bargain and scrimp to make sure the household had everything it needed. If not, there would be hell to pay, and she—along with her mother—would suffer the consequences. She went shopping at Wal-Mart at 3:00 or 4:00 in the morning so as to not run into any of their friends. At home, they ate off paper plates and used plastic utensils and cups to save money on water and dishes. He had a timer for water, and she had to hang clothes in the basement to dry in the winter and outside in the summer. When they had friends over, the clothesline turned into a covering or tent.

Tired of living like a peasant and being embarrassed when people came over, Gloria asked him if she could get a job. He only agreed after he discussed it with his accountant, and then he started making Gloria pay for the household groceries, and that is when the changes started.

Chapter 11: Beth, the Religious Lady

The positive of religion is that it is always there, and it is free. It costs nothing to believe, to say a prayer at the beginning of the day and at the end of the day.

Many people profess to have faith. Do you know how to tell which person is a true believer? It is the person whose mouth is closed. This person lived by the book and abided by the book. I once worked with a person who always touted family values and how his family spent every Sunday in Church. Yet, this person had no scruples and felt perfectly justified in stealing time, stealing money, and taking credit for the work of others. He had the faith all right, the faith to make you want to take the holy spirit to them.

Charles touted his family values, but he should take a page out of Beth's book.

Not one staff member had a negative comment about Beth, nor did they dare try to force her hand at anything. Beth was one of those rare treasures who knew her job, wasn't afraid to do it, and did it with a smile. I'm not saying that she was a pushover because she could hold her own when confronted. But Beth did it without foul language or aggressive body language.

I always wondered at her smile and whether she had any secrets (including what made her tick). She confided that, once you have stepped through fire and have another on your side, there is nothing to fear from man. She gave me shivers with that short paragraph, and whatever demons she had battled were between her and another. However, I knew they had to be bad, for she never wore anything but long skirts, and her arms were covered to the elbows in summer and wrists in the winter.

Before I left, Beth sat down with me in the deserted staff lounge and began by stating, "Sometimes you have to make hard decisions and live hard before you can enjoy life." When I asked what she meant, she said that she was born to a mother who preached religion by day but consumed her nights with members of the church. Some were married, and some were not. Beth believed her mother suffered from depression, but, in her world and her community, mental illness was not openly discussed. She had no knowledge of her father and said she long ago gave up searching for him when she took up the faith. Beth spent years being angry with her mother and others who did not see she was a child in need. She ran away from home at 15 and lived on the streets for many years. When I asked how she survived, she would only reply, "Through the grace of God." Beth disclosed that she was able to leave the streets at the age of 23 due to the kindness of a stranger. I sensed that this person was still involved in her life as she would smile when talking about him and only had positive things to say.

I asked her, "How can you be so forgiving of others when they don't deserve it or continue to do nasty deeds?" She didn't answer.

I also, wanted to know why she had decided at that moment to speak with me and share some of her history, but she would only shrug her shoulders. We had a nice lunch, and, when I could, I would try to eat with her if it were only the two of us. Usually the conversation was light, and we would laugh about the television shows we had in common. Beth always remained the person that she was, and she continued long after I left.

I never did find out why she wore long sleeves and long skirts, but I knew she didn't dress like that out of religious conviction as she made a point of saying that she was like everybody else who had faults and dislikes. Once, she did remark that she missed wearing tank tops in the summer, but— after seeing the expression of her face—I pretended not to hear.

"If the world hates you, ye know that it hated me before it hated you." – John 15:18

Chapter 12: Sarah, the Needy Woman

Sarah was the whiniest, most needy woman you will ever meet. If someone had a new computer she wanted one also. If she found out that free pens were left for staff, she would bitch and complain if she did not get one.

How she graduated from nursing school remains a complex mystery. She couldn't do shit, wouldn't do shit, and expected you to shit for her. Her main goal in life was avoiding work. If you introduced her to a new concept, you had to expect to provide her with extensive hands-on training while answering a million questions. And you could forget about getting her to take notes as she would always ask you to "Show me one more time."

Colleagues held her in low esteem because she always tried to get out of work. If one of her co-workers called in sick, she was on the phone requesting assistance before the start of her shift and before she had access to the patient census. Once, due to karma, the holiday, a full moon, or something, the census dropped to four patients on her side of the unit. She had the assistance of another nurse but *still* called and requested additional help. Some nurses refused to work with her and even switched to the night shift to avoid her.

But, with patients, she would listen to their trial and tribulations for long periods of time. Oh, she would not bathe them, as this was beneath her, but she did have a gentle ear. She especially liked those who were well connected since she always wanted to be a part of the elite society. Her second husband afforded her comforts, but he did not make enough or wasn't powerful enough to be a part of the in crowd. Sarah loved going to plays and concerts where she could pretend that she was part of high society.

Despite her wants, she did love her husband to pieces and thought he walked on water. She considered herself happy but pushed for more. When she found out her friend had built a new house, she told her husband she wanted to move into a bigger house, even though they didn't need the space—they had adult children who rarely visited. Her husband agreed to her request, on the condition that she produce half of the down payments. She was happy to comply, but her co-workers felt as if hell had come to earth because she was always going on and on about it..

Sarah was the one who reported everyone and everything from the maintenance man who looked suspicious to the unit secretaries who spent time on the phone for personal phone calls. When reporting these people, she forgot to report that, if the hospital would do an audit of her home, they would find toilet tissue, cleaning supplies, a walker, wheel chair, packs of paper, and a filing cabinet. She would pretend she had to work late for documentation purposes but her real intent was to make sure no one would notice the items she was placing in her vehicle. Sarah even had the audacity to steal toothpaste and toothbrushes. She kept these items in her bathroom so guests would not notice.

Sarah had a daughter and son. Both were married to individuals who made them happy. They were not rich, but their needs are met. Sarah could not understand this concept and tried to push her daughter into persuading her husband to get a better position with better pay. He did! After the birth of their daughter, he packed up his family and moved several hundreds of miles away. He could have taken something closer, but he felt they needed to get away. Far away!

And who could blame him? Sarah's children avoided her because she constantly solicited their attention, and, if the focus was not on her, she would get angry. When her daughter was in labor, Sarah complained bitterly that she had back pains and that it was unfair of her daughter to go into labor the same day she was experiencing pains.

Going out to eat with Sarah was a challenge because the food was never the way she wanted it to be. At one restaurant, she complained about a salad fork that was chilled, which she didn't want to be. Then the salad appeared to be missing some lettuce.

If I were her, I would have left without eating a thing. At another restaurant (I heard), the management informed her that she could not return to their establishment under any circumstances.

And it wasn't just restaurants that displeased Sarah—or whom she displeased. She returned the same bedroom set to a furniture store three times until the store manager told her to either keep the set or return it to the store for a full refund. She decided to keep it, but she bitched to anyone who would listen that she felt ripped off.

Sarah got along famously with physicians, who thought of her as a go-getter. She won a nurse's award for best bedside manner, and she left the facility when a physician offered her the opportunity to manage his office. I did not understand!!!

Chapter 13: Vickie ("I Know Some-one; That's How I Got a Job")

Vickie slid off the pole and slid into a cushion position with her g-string still in her hand. Tired of men groping her and showing her goodies for $20.00 or less, Vickie went back to school to earn her degree. She was a quick learner and was able to pass tests by memorizing terms and concepts, but she could not apply what she had learned. When she was in school, she often paid others to write her papers, a win-win situation that benefited all parties involved, as far as she was concerned.

The problem with Vickie was that she still showed her goodies but for a higher rate and only when it benefited her. She had an uncle whose friend was a member of the hospital board. Telling him that she wanted to change her life, she convinced her uncle to get her a job. And not just any job. Vickie landed a job that paid well over $45,000 a year plus benefits. Vickie loved her job, but she was dumb as a post.

Vickie made many mistakes, such as completing the wrong paperwork for transfers and informing family members of a patient's condition when she was not supposed to. The only reason Vickie was not fired was because Alex covered up her mistakes (because she had a direct link to the powers that be). Vickie didn't care what others thought. She came to work when she wanted to and always left before five. She once commented that she could not work past four as her brain just shut down and her body needed time to readjust for the next day.

Vickie was dangerous; she was an enormous flirt and showed particular attention to male patients and male employees. Rumor had it that she had even slept with two co-workers at the same time while eating a cucumber. It could have been true; you really did not know with Vickie,

Since I was not a male nor did I have any power to get her what she wanted, I did not exist in her world—except when we bumped heads, which was frequently. I don't know when the change happened, but one day she accused me of scaring off her client from treatment, an absurd accusation because everyone knew I was an advocate for treatment, but I also knew that threatening and intimidating people into taking treatment (including threatening to take away the patient's child) could cause the opposite effect, which is exactly what happened.

She stopped me in the hall by blocking my entrance and asking if she could speak with me. I politely told her no, but she persisted. "I think we need to speak now!" she said.

"What can't wait?"

"My patient" she screeched.

So as to not cause a scene, I asked if we could step into the hall closet, which was small but gave us both enough space so that we did not have to touch each other or breathe each other's air.

"Listen, you, I don't know who you are, but, when I tell a patient they have to go to therapy, then that's what going to happen!" she yelled, pointing her finger in my face.

"First, you are going to get your finger out of my face, and, second, we don't threaten patients through their children. There are other ways to engage clients in treatment. If the child is abused or mistreated, then that warrants a call to child-protective services, but not if she is depressed and let the child eat cereal for dinner but had the foresight to call her mother to come get the child so the girl would not witness her crying."

"Shut up, shut up, you despicable person!"

"This conversation is over,"" I said and turned to open the door. She snatched at my hand. I slapped her hand away and again to attempt to open the door. She hit my hand with her fist and threatened, "I am going to tell, and you won't have a job tomorrow. They only hired you—"

That was the last thing she said, for I had had enough. I grabbed her by throat, pushed my face into hers and told her not to say another word and not to ever threaten me.

She was as shocked as was I by my behavior, but I could not take any more from someone who slid down a pole and slid into a job just because she knew someone but lacked the experience or the intelligence to perform the duties required. After that confrontation, she wore a scarf around her neck the next day, and we never exchange words unless we needed to discuss a patient, and, from that point on, she valued and respected my input. The delivery was wrong, and I was wrong, but it solved a whole lot of problems.

Chapter 14: Enough Is Enough

I stayed on that job for five long years. During that time, Alex left after inheriting a large sum of money and property. Right after he left, it was revealed that monies had been mismanaged and some staff did not have the required credentials. Guess Alex wasn't at smart as he thought he was.

Liz was still married to her husband, and he was still having extra-marital affairs, except now his children from those affairs wanted to be involved in his life and he had begun to pressure Liz about having family gatherings so they could all be one big happy family. She thought he had lost his mind, but no way was she going to give up the benefits he had and the life-insurance policies. She heard about women divorcing their men and how the second wife lived grandly and in splendor while the first had to deal with lonely men with no benefits who were looking for women to take care of them. Unbeknownst to Liz, he changed one of the policies to include his children. Dig one ditch, dig two.

Hilary and Charles ended up having an affair, but she left him after he found out she was involved with a client. Since she knew Charles' secrets as well as he knew hers, he did not expose her, and she continues to practice today. Hilary dropped her therapist and no longer let her family borrow money from her or use her to baby-sit. Her family blamed her new boyfriend, and, when Hilary got tired of the blame, she and the boyfriend left the state without giving her family their new address.

Dr. Riley's wife left him for a younger man who was penniless and drove a garbage truck. Yet she smiled every day because he treated her like a queen. They had to scrimp and save for everything, but she was gloriously happy and gloriously pregnant with their first child (a girl). Soon after the divorce, the doctor remarried. He married a girl who worked for a pharmaceutical company. She had her own money and did not take any shit from him. They were neither happy nor sad.

Vickie quit after she married a doctor and rumor had it she got plastic surgery and now resembled some actress. She vowed to never strip or work again.

Beth continued to let her faith guide her and will probably outlast the cockroaches in the building.

Me, I left something that I loved. But the people needed more help than the clients, and I often wondered why they let the staff have the keys instead of the patients. Off to the races for another job hunt.

Chapter 15: The Family Business: Shelly, Born into Money

What the hell was I thinking? I met Shelly at a temp agency. She was there to meet with management to discuss an open position. Lively and easy to talk to, she sat beside me while I was completing an application and mentioned the job to me. It was with her family business. Her family was in the business of monitoring people with alert buttons. Their patients pushed a button, and the company responded with phone calls and, if necessary, it sent the police or an ambulance to the client's door. Shelly said the position offered great benefits, and decent pay. My job would be to monitor those who answered the phones and, when problems weren't solved, to take the calls myself. Easy, right? *Hell no!* Those people like to drove me to my former job—as a patient—and I learned a valuable lesson: Never work for a small family business when the family does not get along.

On the day I met Shelly and she offered me the job, she forgot to mention that there really wasn't any open position nor was the company supposed to spend money on another employee. *Shelly* was supposed to work the supervisor position. After all, she was drawing a salary and spent less than 10 hours a week on the job. When her brother asked her about this, her reply was, "I'm marketing. How do you think people learn about us?"

The company consisted of Shelly, who was vice president; her brother, the president; a step sister, who was the accountant; Shelly's husband, the maintenance man; and their mother, who helped out when needed. Because the family was cheap, to save money, they gave nobody outside of the family except me a full-time position. You can imagine my surprise when I found this out, and you can imagine what everyone felt about me my first week on the job. But it turned out it didn't matter as, for some reason, Shelly took a liking to me and I became her confidant. I think she had a twisted view of our "friendship" and thought of herself as a character out of an old Southern novel.

Shelly was married to a man much younger than she, and she was always spending money trying to keep up with him or to look as young as he. She spent thousands of dollars on cosmetics and worked out extensively to keep her body in shape. She ate desserts only on special occasions and limited herself to two glasses of wine per day, no exceptions. Shelly wanted plastic surgery but she was deathly afraid of needles or being disfigured or dying if the surgery went wrong.

I knew her obsession with makeup, and one day I had to come in at the crack of dawn because a staff member had called in sick. The section that housed their cubicles was on a different floor of the building. It was dark, and I was searching for the light switch when I heard a panicky voice yell, "Don't scream; it's me!" I couldn't scream or form words or thoughts. I stood on the stairwell shaking like an idiot. Shelly flicked on the light, and I *did* scream. She had no eyebrows, no lips, and something was funky with her hair.

"What the fuck?"

"I didn't put my makeup on yet."

"No shit! What happened?" I asked.

"I have to drawn in my eyebrows every day because of a botched bleach job, and I need to plump up my lips with lipstick and liner. As for the hair, I wear wigs." After I got past the lips and eyebrows, I could see that her hair wasn't that bad. It probably would be cute with the right color and cut and might even take years off her face. I told her this, and she pulled out her mirror and began to examine herself the way a physician would. That woman had a critical eye for skin and makeup, but hair was outside of her realm. "Hmm," she murmured. "I think you might be right. Promise you won't tell anyone what I look like without makeup."

"Who cares?"

"I care, and will you not tell?"

"Okay, but don't sneak up on me. …How long does it take you to get dressed?"

"At least an hour or two, depending on the function and the day."

"So, if you have to be at work at 7:00 in the morning, you are up at—what?—5 a.m.?"

"No, 4:30." She was crazy as hell!

For all the time and money she spent on her looks, it didn't matter to her husband, Matt. He loved Shelly, and he loved older women, and Shelly had him by 10 years. Well, she said 10, but Shelly actually was 15 years older than Matt—and now he wanted a child. She was afraid that he would find out her real age and afraid of what a child would do to her body.

Chapter 16: The Family Business: Brother David (Like Father, Like Son)

Shelly's brother, David, was tired. He was tired of his wife, Kim, who only talked of babies and how bad she wanted one. His sister and her husband were another thorn in his side that required constant monitoring. David's mother only wanted money from the company and to not have to be involved in the day-to-day operations. David's father started the business many years ago with a dream and little support from his spouse. In actuality, it was his father's mistress who dreamed of the idea and convinced him to go into business. The mistress was smart: she made him give her 15% ownership, and she had it done legally via an attorney. Every month, the mistress, along with David's mother, received a stipend. "How stupid can one man be?" he repeatedly asked himself.

David thought of Kim, whom he married when he was young and foolish. Oh, he believed she loved him and he loved her, but their love was like a pot simmering on the stove. It was a low heat, and it took forever to cook. He, like his father before him, had a mistress. Unlike his father, he did not put his mistress in his will. However, he did shower her with gifts (which included paying for her home and giving her money whenever she asked for it or he felt like giving some to her). His mistress fulfilled a need and provided a passion that he couldn't control. Their affair had lasted more than 15 years. He could not give her up, nor could he give in to his wife's demand to have a child.

David didn't care if Kim ever got pregnant because that would affect his relationship with his mistress. Thinking of his mistress, he called her on his cell phone and made plans to meet her for dinner.

David gave Kimberly free reign with the office and staff, and she made sure everyone knew that she was the boss's wife and therefore the boss. She was the only family member who was truly interested in the business. And she knew that, if she and David ever divorced, she would not be able to continue to do what she loved. David knew it, too. So she stuck by him. And David knew—because she wanted to remain an active member of the business—that she would always be there for him, whether they had kids or not.

Chapter 17: Martha—the Other Kind

Martha had the worst habit. She spoke of people and would whisper things like, "You know how *they* are." When you asked who *they* were, she would reply "You know: the *other* kind."

From what I could figure out, the other kind was anybody who did not think, act, or look like Martha. She always prided herself on "being equal." yet she could not define *equal* nor did she care to explain her remarks. After working with her, I had no idea of who the other kind was—nor did I care. In fact, no one cared but her, and even her family ignored her to the point of rudeness or exclusion. She was the special child who, they concluded, had to be look after.

It was rumored that, years ago, she smoked too many of those "left-handed cigarettes," which left her too few left-handed brain cells. This was her tenth job in less than seven years, and she knew it was a matter of time before she lost this job because of her family. Martha had a daughter, Roberta, who ran away from home at the age of 13. Despite the fact that Martha filed a missing-person report and got the police, her family, and her friends involved in the search, no one could locate the child. Then, ten years later Roberta reappeared. She was the complete opposite of what she had been and demanded to be called Lexus (like the car) because she was luxurious and expensive. Martha had no idea what she meant, and she was afraid to ask too many questions. Lexus refused to talk about what her drove her away or what brought her back. But after staying in town for a few years, she left again without leaving a note or making a phone call.

You would think, because it bothered Martha and gave her nightmares that her only child was estranged from her, that she would be nicer and more sympathetic to others, yet, instead, she managed to be nasty and condescending to those around her. To ease her pain she smoked her left handers and talked about "the *other* kind." After all, the eleventh job was around the corner.

Chapter 18: The Family Business: The Bitch for No Reason

Kimberly, David's spouse, prided herself on her appearance and education. Kim, as she was called by her friends, wanted a baby so bad, but, after 20 years of trying, she was not able to conceive, nor was she approved for adoption. She did not want an older child, which made adoption extremely difficult; she had her heart set on a baby. Kim wanted to try a private adoption, but her husband did not want to spend that kind of money, and she could not convince him otherwise.

On the job, Kim was despised by all she came into contact with because she used her position as the boss's wife to make others do her bidding and to fire those who didn't. She woke up in the morning with a frown and went to bed (alone, many nights) with a frown. Kim did not drink her troubles away because she still held out hope of adoption. After all, she was only 42, and people still adopted 'way past 45. The one thing Kim did not want do was consult a fertility specialist, for she knew why she could not conceive and she didn't want her husband to find out: at the age of 16, she got pregnant and had an abortion. Kim did not want to abort, but her mother forced her. Her mother was marrying a new man (her third), and she informed Kim that a baby would ruin her reputation along with her body. Kim's husband either did not care or wasn't concerned enough to question her continued barren state. The one time she suggested a surrogate, he nearly ripped her to shreds, and the matter was dropped.

This is why Kim gave the staff hell—especially when she would see pictures of their families, sometimes with multiple children, on their desks. Out of spite, she banned all pictures. Kimberly was spiteful for another reason as well. Her childhood friend who knew her secret had returned to town, and they now traveled in the same circles. She was deathly afraid that her friend would reveal the secret reason why she could not have children.

Chapter 19: Clara ("Let Me Bake You Something!")

Clara was the one reason among many why I never eat food offered by any co-workers. Not that I think I am any safer with restaurant food, but at least, with a restaurant, I can more easily pinpoint the source of my poison, and the health department can ensure that the establishment does not repeat the same mistakes twice.

Clara had been married for 16 years and decided to return to work part time once her teenage daughter and son entered high school. The extra money helped to pay for household items, vacations, and emergencies. Clara always had a peculiar odor about her—not an unclean aroma but one you could not identify. At times, it reminded me of cloves; other times I could not determine the scent. She always had a smile and a kind word for you, and, at the holidays, she brought in homemade goodies which everyone raved about. A few times, she was paid to make pastries. She enjoyed doing it and prided herself on her good luck.

Yet Clara was nasty, nasty, nasty. Once, I encountered her in the restroom, and I almost lost it.

I was at the sink washing my hands when she came out of the stall. She proceeded to fluff her hair, then the nastiest thing she did was scratch her privates, smell her hand, and say, "A girl can't be too sure."

She was about to leave the restroom when I intercepted her. "Clara, you need to wash your hands!"

"Why?"

"You just used the restroom and scratched!"

Ignoring me, she left, leaving me staring out after her.

I, being who I am, could not let it go. I followed her out to her desk and requested to speak with her in private. We went into the employee's break-room. "Carla, I do not mean to demean or offend you, but, if what I witnessed in the bathroom is a part of your routine, then it may be best if you don't bring in food for others to consume. I am not telling you what to do; I am asking you. Germs spread. I'm not claiming that you have a disease or anything. It is just that our bodies produce elements that should not be combined with food, and, while you may not think it's harmful, think of how many people touch the restroom doors—or the refrigerator for that matter."

She looked at me and replied, "I don't like being harassed!"

"Excuse me?"

"You are harassing me," she repeated.

"I am not, I would like to think we are having a private conversation, and, although it may be embarrassing and uncomfortable, it's about something that needs to be addressed."

Carla's face took on another dimension, and she replied that she was leaving and did not want me to follow or speak to her unless it was business related.

I left the break room and forgot about the conversation because we became extremely busy and I ended up staying later than usual. The next day, Kimberly approached me and informed me that she needed to speak with me immediately. She told me this in front of several employees who raised their eyebrows at my predicament.

Inside her husband's office, she asked me to sit and began by stating, "We are a company that prides itself on being professional and courteous. If this does not happen, then we may cease to exist or our revenue could decrease, which could result in the loss of employees. Do you understand what I am saying?"

"Actually, I don't." I was totally confused by her statement and her demeanor.

"Listen," she continued," Carla complained and reported you for harassing her. Is it true?"

"No, I simply pulled her aside to speak with her privately after witnessing some disturbing behavior."

"Did this behavior have anything to do with the work environment?"

"Well—" I began but she cut me off.

"Carla informed me of the bathroom incident, and, while I did not agree with her antics, it has nothing to do with her work or production. I know you have a background in social services, but you need to leave you bleeding heart at the door and remember no one wants to live like you do, nor it is in the best interest for you to repeat this or try to analyze Carla. Am I understood?

"Perfectly"

I left the office fuming and ran into Carla carrying a foil-covered dish into the break room. She continued to bake, and I made sure to not touch anything she touched, and my stack of sanitizers and usage of same increased.

Chapter 20: Sheila, the Sexy One

Sheila wore three-inch heels to work every day, and her makeup was perfect. Her clothing was expensive, and she had a habit of letting everyone know the cost of her apparel and how she came to acquire her wardrobe. Sheila had a natural approach to the opposite sex, and she liked to brag about how good she was at getting what she wanted because men were basically dumb and fell for the girl who always put in the extra effort. She usually made this statement while glancing around the room at other women or men.

Sheila was conceited, but, she was honest. She informed whomever she dated that she was not interested in marriage or long-term relationships and that she expected to be courted and to be frequently showered with presents—*nice* presents. She did not apologize for her behavior. Grown men used to beg her not to leave and on many occasions, would send flowers and expensive gifts to her at the office. If she was no longer involved with the guy, she would leave the flowers for her colleagues.

Sheila had one Achilles heel, and that was her mother. She and her mother were very close, and, no matter what, she always took her mother's calls.

Once you knew the circumstances of Sheila's early life, you could understand why and how she grew up the way she did. Sheila was born very poor. Her father worked very hard to support Sheila and her younger brother (four years her junior), but there was never enough money, and often dinner would be a mayonnaise sandwich with a banana—or just plain bread. Sheila did not like school because the other girls would tease her for being poor or for wearing clothing that was out of style or barely hanging on.

Sheila's mother had asthma, and her attacks would land her in the hospital. Even with medical insurance, the family experienced thousands of dollars' worth of medical bills. When Sheila was 14, in order to get a job, she lied about her age and, by stealing the stamp from the guidance counselor's office, forged the school counselor's signature. The man who hired her did not care because he was able to pay her lower wages for the same work. Sheila swept floors, cleaned bathrooms, emptied trash cans, and stocked shelves. The money she earned helped the family, and they were able to have meat more often. However, after she'd been on the job for less than six months, her father suffered a massive heart attack. The family had no life insurance, and he was buried in a plain box.

Sheila continued to work for the same employer, and, as time went by, he increased her pay and even gave her bonuses during the holidays. By the time she was 16, she had blossomed into a beauty, and the boys were paying attention. After one boy took her out to eat (the first time she'd been to a fancy restaurant) and gave her a card with $50.00 in it, she realized the value of what she had. The money went to her mother, and she made sure to take leftovers to her mother and brother.

She did graduate from high school, but, with no one to guide or encourage her; she went on to work a series of odd jobs while dating. As she got older, her dates became even more devoted to her and had deeper pockets. It was also during this time that her brother became distraught over a relationship gone bad and hung himself. Shelia convinced her boyfriend at the time to pay for the funeral. It was later revealed that the girl her brother was involved with was pregnant. She came to Sheila's mother's home while the mother was out and asked for money. Sheila slammed the door in her face and began the process of getting enough money to move her mother out of their present circumstances.

Another of her admirers always discussed stocks and, although he bored her to tears, taught her the value and importance of saving, and she now had a hefty bank account along with several stock options. Her colleagues thought she was materialistic, vain, and dumb. They were right about two out of the three, wrong about the most important one: she wasn't dumb, not by a long shot. Sheila was probably the only person at the company who could afford *not* to work.

Chapter 21: Brad ("I Don't Mind Working")

Brad was a man who worked and worked hard. If someone called in sick and you needed to get a replacement, he was your man. He would come in on his day off. He never complained about the work, and he came to work with a packed lunch box and little notes inside the box. He never shared the contents of the notes, and he rarely spoke of his family except when asked directly, and then he would answer in short, clipped sentences. Brad was not rude, just abrupt.

Brad would engage in conversation—would chat or smile—but would not share private thoughts. That's because Brad had learned a hard lesson about office politics and gossip. Several years ago, the company he worked for closed amidst much mismanagement and gossip. At the time, many of his co-workers resented him because he was the lead supervisor and had inside knowledge of impeding layoffs. Brad was caught in a bind; he had worked with many of his colleagues for a lot of years and felt bad for them and their families, but he could not disclose what he knew. He was doubly unfortunate because he was let go along with the same colleagues he had tried to protect and, for a period of time, had to endure their nasty phone calls and vandalism. (He had his tires slashed more than once.) After a year of no work, he obtained this job and later on picked up a second job as a warehouse supervisor. The money he made was enough to support his family, but Brad closed himself off from others at work and made no friends, nor did he make enemies.

It was during their hard times that his spouse informed him that she was pregnant with their fourth child. They had to borrow from his parents and hers to survive. After he had been working three years on both jobs, Brad and his family were beginning to dig themselves out of their financial hole. He liked some of his colleagues and thought Kimberly was the real reason the company was successful, as she knew the ins and outs of the business and spent a lot of time learning every job and every employee. He knew she was hated, but secretly he admired her for not giving a damn about what people thought of her.

Brad admired Kimberly because he used to be Kimberly in another job, another position, another life. He liked to think of himself as someone who was fair and cared for his employees, but that was far from the truth. He once was ordered to lay off an employee, and, instead of doing it behind closed doors, he walked up to the man and informed him that his services were no longer needed and told him to gather his things. He fired the employee in such a public manner in order to prove a point and to show other employees what could happen when you did not abide by his rules. In that other job, Brad would walk around with a clipboard containing a list of each employee. If he happened upon you while you were engaging in a private conversation or some other activity that was an infraction of the rules, he would mark it down and use it against you come evaluation time. He was rewarded with trips and cash bonuses for his ability to keep costs down in his department and save the company money. Brad usually achieved these goals by targeting those who had been employed for years because they were drawing the highest salaries, so, if they went, the company could save money by replacing them with a less-expensive new person. He loved his job and walked around like he was a king.

When he lost his job, he was devastated because he had thought he was so important. Brad did not know it, but, the day he was laid off, his former employees and even his colleagues went to a bar and toasted his demise. The worst part of it for Brad was that a person he had considered to be his friend took over his job.

Brad suffered greatly at home when he lost his job. His family lost status within their circle, and they had to downsize a lot. The new vehicle his wife bought with the personalized plates was traded in for a small economical car. The five-bedroom house was sold for a three-bedroom house with a small backyard and no swimming pool. Gone too were the credit cards with limits of $5,000 or more. Brad's wife learned to shop at discount and warehouse stores. She did not like the idea of being poor and told him on countless occasions that he was the man and he was supposed to take care of her and, by that, she did not mean in the current state of finances. Every day she put a note in his box which read, "Remember your promise, and you are better than this. Love."

Chapter 22: Elise ("I Am Only Working Here Until I Get My Degree")

Elise was determined and goal oriented. She was a single mother, attending school while raising her daughter. The child's father paid no support, and she did not request it of him. Her philosophy was, if he wanted to be a man and take care of his child, then he should want to do it, not be made to do it. Elise made sure that her child did not suffer while she worked part time and took classes. She made up her for her lack of funds by taking out student loans and getting whatever scholarships she could. She refused to get public assistance, but she paid a fortune to get insurance for herself and her daughter. Every month, Elise wondered how she was going to make it. Due to the stress in her life, Elise cursed like a sailor. She vowed to quit but could not; after all, she had been cursing since she was a child. She did not drink because she grew up around alcoholics and was afraid letting the disease have the power. Elise had less than a year left of school, and she was determined to graduate on schedule.

Elise as usual was running late, and, naturally, her daughter wanted oatmeal instead of cereal and complained about not having juice to go with her morning breakfast. Then, when she was putting on her child's sneakers, Elise noticed that they had a tear, so she spent another ten minutes going though shoes that her daughter had either outgrown or did not approve of. "Shit, shit, shit," she said." Upon getting the look from her daughter, Elise tried to make amends by yelling, "Damn!" This produced a smile from her daughter.

To make matters worse—this was the real reason she was late—her ex decided to call as she was looking for her keys.

"Else?" he asked as soon as she answered the phone.

"What the hell do you want?"

"Nice to hear from you too, darling."

Rolling her eyes, distracted by the task she was performing, Elise prompted him to get to the point and state the reason for his phone call.

"My mother and I want Shelly to come out here for a visit."

"You can kiss all four sides of my ass! You barely call and have not paid any support in I don't know how long. Not only is the answer 'Hell, no!' but you can go to Hell also."

"She is six, Elise, and she is old enough to say if she wants to visit or not."

"Then take me to court, and, while you are at it, you can explain to the judge why you have not paid child support, contributed to my college fund, bought clothes for our kid, paid for medical insurance or even bought her a happy meal, you spineless fuck." After throwing those words at him, she slammed the phone down and hollered for Shelly, "Let's go!"

Elise's morning got worse after she met with one of her advisors regarding graduation. Tuition was in less than a month, and she had to pay it at the same time her rent and insurance were due. Elise could get more hours at work, but that would mean working at night, and she did not trust anyone to babysit her child. While Elise worked during the day, Shelly stayed at school for the aftercare program.

Elise thought of this as she was hurrying into the building to clock in for work. She ran into Carla, who was carrying a covered dish. Elise greeted Carla and complimented her on her cooking but mentally patted herself on the back for not eating anything Carla brought into to work. She had overheard the conversation in the bathroom, where she had had her feet propped against the wall while studying for a test. Some people were just filthy nasty, which meant they were nastier than filth. This job taught Elise lots of lessons about what happens in the work place and what not to become involved in. The truth was, she did not have time as she had to worry about raising her daughter, paying bills, getting her degree, finding another job, and remaining sane. As she always told her daughter, "Do you!"—a phrase she always used, which means, "Take care of yourself."

Chapter 23: Alice, the Invisible One

No one paid Alice any attention at work or at home. Alice hated cleaning up at home, then coming to work to clean up after people who were supposed to be adults and who should know that toilets should be flushed, food should be taken out of the microwave, and a full trash bin should be emptied. Why should they need to wait for her to do it? But it was a job. And it wasn't all bad because a lot of the time she was on her own.

She cleaned the offices from 4:00 in the afternoon until 9:00 at night. She liked working after 6:00, when most employees were gone. She did not like the hours before 6:00: that was the time she had to clean Ms. Kimberly and Mr. David's office. Neither one of them paid any attention to her except when she missed something or they wanted something cleaned in addition to the usual.

Sometimes, Ms. Kimberly would shake her empty coffee cup at Alice to indicate she wanted a refill. Once Kimberly even sent someone to look for Alice so Alice could get her a cup of coffee. In the time it took for the employee to find Alice and for the energy Kimberly exerted on the search, Kimberly could have poured her own damn coffee. Alice could not tell you how many times she thought of spitting in the cups she brought to Kimberly, but she refrained by repeating to herself that Ms. Kimberly was miserable. She heard her on the phone talking about her female problems and how badly she wanted a baby. Alice also knew of David's affair and how he had no respect for his sister and brother in law. That's because they would discuss private issues in front of Alice as if she had no ears and no heart.

Since, they made no effort to temper their conversations, Alice knew things that no one else was privy to but who was she to tell and why? Maybe that's why they never bothered to censor their thoughts because they knew that Alice had no one to tell or no one to listen to her. Her husband was involved with their teenage sons, and, if an issue did not concern sports or mechanics, he had no interest. Conversation between him and Alice consisted of talking about the household bills, what was for dinner, and who would drive the kids where on the weekend. He never asked her if she liked her job, was satisfied, or enjoyed her work. In truth, Alice wanted to go to school to become a nurse, but her husband discouraged her, claiming they could not afford it and that, at 34, she was too old for school. After unsuccessfully bringing it up, she let the subject drop but continued to harbor secret dreams. She even went to a local technical college to inquire if they taught anything in the medical field.

Now Alice had a secret of her own. Tired of hearing her husband say no and her eager to change her life, she had enrolled in a program at the technical college and started attending classes several months ago. Alice took courses in the morning while the children were in school and her husband was at work. No one thought to ask how she spent her mornings. Alice had rented a post-office box to have information from the school sent to her, and she kept her books inside the trunk of her car under the spare tire. She studied at work and completed homework assignments there. usually after 9:00 p.m., when her shift was finished. She loved working in Kimberly's office as it was quiet and away from prying eyes.

Kimberly and David were not only ones who thought of Alice as being invisible. Only two people at work took the time to talk to her. I thought I was the only one, but it turned out that Kimberly had someone who saw Alice for what she was and the potential she had. This person would talk to her and offer encouragement. Alice never divulged her inner thoughts, but she got the feeling that this person understood her inner turmoil and her dreams.

Alice did not like keeping secrets from her husband and planned to tell him about school, but she decided to keep the post-office box. And she definitely intended to continue with school. She liked being in an atmosphere where people encouraged her to engage in conversation and asked her opinion. It was so different from "What's for dinner?"

Chapter 24: Beatrice ("I Got the Job Due to Friendship!")

Beatrice arrived to work bright and early one day. No one knew she was coming, and no one knew she had been hired. I approached her and, upon questioning her, discovered Kimberly had hired her. I learned later on that Beatrice was the daughter of one of Kimberly's friends; Kimberly had hired her as a favor to her friend. She had no experience and no practical knowledge of how an office worked.

I was extremely pissed as I had to train her, and I could tell by glances thrown my way that others were worrying about their jobs and wondering if her hours would cut into theirs. Just what the hell I needed! Who in the hell named their child Beatrice anyway in this day and time? Why give the poor thing that name when what you imagine is exactly what you get? Beatrice did not try—with her appearance or anything. Bland would be the perfect adjective to describe her. Many times, it appeared as if she rolled out of bed, into her clothes, and into work. Her hair would stand up in odd places, and, when you spoke with her, you found yourself tilting your head to fit her hair into range. Her hair was actually gorgeous, and many would probably have envied her for it if she took either comb or brush to it. I was angry about how she got the job, but a part of me pitied her because I knew that sooner rather than later it would come to a bitter end.

Within a week, Beatrice looked around her cubicle and found Brad staring at her. She could not imagine what he was thinking but figured it was not good thoughts. She turned to her side and found Elise looking at her, but she did manage a thin smile.

Beatrice felt out of place, and she hated this job. The only reason she took it was on account of the pressure from her parents, who insisted she do *something* since she had flunked out of two schools and bitterly protested that she did not want to go to a third nor did she want to go to work. However, because she had no job skills and no income, she had to abide by their rules. The only pleasure Beatrice got was from food—to make it and to eat it. What she really wanted was to be a chef. When she informed her parents, they made nasty and derogatory remarks about her, which Beatrice refused to repeat to anyone.

Her oddness made her a lonely child, but money has its advantages: since her parents had a lot of it, it allowed her to engage in activities which pleased her If one took the time to learn about Beatrice and earn her trust, she could become a valuable friend.

Beatrice wasn't worried about friends; she was more concerned about what Kimberly had promised her mother: that she would not have to work long in this initial job but would have a supervisory position within the month. She just needed to be train. This was wishful thinking; Beatrice was neither manager nor even supervisor material, but, when one had a personal relationship with the boss, one could do what one wanted.

Chapter 24: The Change

Shelly called me early one morning to say that she and her husband were taking a long cruise to Europe. She also wanted to let me know that I was a great employee and good friend. I found this odd as I did not consider Shelly a friend, but—what the hell—it made her feel good. I continued to focus on training Beatrice, a task which proved to be very challenging. Anybody else who performed (or, rather, *didn't* perform) as she did would have been fired, but I was told not to complain and to continue to work with her in the hopes she would get better.

Three weeks later, the shit hit the fan when Kimberly, along with David, called a mandatory meeting for all employees. This was extremely odd as you rarely saw the two of them together, and they never shared a meeting. "I want to thank everyone for their hard work and want you to know that you are appreciated as individuals and as an asset to this company," Kimberly said. She looked around the room before continuing. "As you are aware, our business has been down, and, even with creative

100 G. C. Smith

budgeting, we had to make some hard choices. Unfortunately those choices include layoffs. This is very hard for us, as we have grown attached to each other and view each other as family. If the business changes and we are able to rehire, then those let go will be the first notified, and we will keep your names and numbers on file. We will provide those who are laid off with one week of severance pay. We wish it could be more, but it can't. I will be speaking with each of you privately regarding the layoff and changes." Turning to David, she asked if he had anything to add. He said no. Kimberly grabbed his hand and they exited together.

I stood there like a fool for several minutes before I could find my voice. In less than five minutes people's lives had changed. What would people do? I felt sorry for those who were about to lose their jobs, and I was mentally preparing for the reference-letter writing and the tears. Carla was already crying, and Elise looked shell shocked. I could not gauge Brad's reaction. Sheila was her regular self.

I sat down in my cubicle to gather my thoughts when Kimberly buzzed me. I knew I would be the first she would call in. I approached her door with dread about the names she would provide and how her list would affect me along with everybody else.

I knocked on her door, and she called, "Come in."

Opening the door, I noticed several things. She had redecorated since I was last in her office, and she was alone. I guess David was no longer needed for the drama part. Without any preamble, she began by stating, "I'm sorry, but you are one of those who will be laid off. Since you are at a higher salary than any other employee and full time, letting you go is is a method for saving jobs. David and I spoke, and we agreed to give you a month's severance."

Looking at me, she asked if I had any questions. What do you say when you been fired unexpectedly. "No." I murmured.

She handed me an envelope along with a typed letter of recommendation from David. I tried not to slam the door on my way out. I was mad and frightened, worrying about how I would handle my bills and responsibilities without a job. I silently berated myself for thinking that I wouldn't be the one to lose my job when all the time it *was* me. As I walked to my desk, I noticed co-workers staring at me curiously but refused to engage with them. I began to pack up my belongings, including contact numbers I'd acquired and the training manual I created. *Let them create their own*, I thought nastily. Carla was loudly sobbing, and Beatrice was patting her back. I did not notice when Brad was called in. Nearly choking, I told everybody goodbye and carried my box to my car.

It was not until I was out of the parking lot that I let myself cry. "*No!*" I bawled with heaves and loud sobs. I felt abandoned, abused, and used. *We are like family*. Yeah, right. Cursing at the top of my lungs with every foul and nasty word I could think of, I now realized why Shelly had called me.

Two months later, I was home cleaning and thinking of my future when the phone rang. Not recognizing the number shown by caller ID, I answered the phone expecting a telemarketer. It was Beatrice. "How are you?" she asked.

"I'm fine."

"I know this may seem awkward or odd, but I wanted to call to say thank you for all your help and to let you know you were a great trainer."

"Thank you," I replied, ready to hang up when she continued.

"I left the company and decided to go to culinary school."

"Good for you! I hope you are happy."

She laughed and remarked, "You are the first person to care about my happiness. Before I let you go, I want to say I think it's a shame that they let you go and then made Sheila a manager and key person in the second business they opened."

I could not even hear what type of business it was. My ears were ringing, and I felt dizzy. "Sheila is a manager?"

"Oh, yeah. Brad, Elise, and a few others were let go. Carla left because she had some kind of problem with her stomach. Well, I just wanted to say hi and thank you. I hope you are able to bounce back."

"I always do," I remarked, hanging up the phone.

It was strange but I never ran into any of my old colleagues. However, I used to read about Kimberly, David, and Shelly in the paper whenever they attended charity events or received awards from the city for good business practices. I had to laugh: Sheila turned out to be smarter than I or anybody else gave her credit for. Kimberly never did conceive, nor did she and David adopt. She became an advocate for the local animal shelter, and I came across an article which said she had adopted two dogs. *Poetic justice*, I thought.

I knew what my next step should be and what I wanted to do, but I was scared as I had not only myself to think about but the welfare of others. I decided one day to stop thinking and to just feel, and I made a decision. I thought I had received an education on my previous jobs, but just wait until I achieve a career. Ooh, boy, what's next? I'll give you a hint. It starts with a P and ends in D.

Acknowledgments

Special thanks to the women in my life who offer me unconditional support and love.

To my mother who gave me the gift of laughter and her wicked sense of humor: I will always be a part of you.

To my special girl (my daughter): I like how you try to listen to your better mind and how you have a sense of drive to get things done. You make my day better every day!

To my sister, who is the best mother I know, and who inherited our mother's special skills for decorating, cooking, and doing hair.

To my younger sister, who suggested I write this book a long time ago.

Special thanks to my good friend Maranda for providing me with positive thoughts and for giving me the title for this book.

Lastly, to P.R. who supported me throughout the years and made me realize that things could be worse (smile!!!).